A Life Worthy of Death

I0641175

By
Dommartini Salien Sr.

A Life Worthy of Death

DEDICATION

To my empress K.

Thank you for September.

Dominique is an eight-year-old Haitian kid living a life filled with love, familial support, and adventure. Growing up in a country gripped by severe poverty, desolation, as well as a brutal dictatorship, Dominique still finds ways to experience the beauties of life. As he navigates the common challenges of adolescence, he must also overcome the greater barriers that awaits him in his future.

With a budding puppy love, a mysterious dream that keeps showing him a vision he can't understand, and a government regime that is threating to kill his father, will he have enough strength to endure?

"Easter egg hunt: Awesome reader, every chapter of this novel has one bold word each. Take each of those words and fill them in the blank spaces at the end of the book to find out what the thematic question is for you to answer in the given empty space. In order to for you to find those words, you gotta read! :-) Good luck."

TABLE OF CONTENTS

ACKNOWLEDGEMENT

ACKNOWLEDGEMENT

"To all of those individuals who played a role in my life story, good, bad, and ugly, thank you."

A Life Worthy of Death

~ Chapter 1~

L'Union Fait La Force

(Strength in Unity)

"ARRRGGHHH, HELP ME, IT HURTS! IT
HURTS, PLEASE HELP!"

I woke up startled and sat straight up in my cot,
completely drenched in sweat. The moon's long leg
still beamed through the shanty's window onto my
sheet covers. I looked over from my little cot and
saw my family was still fast asleep. Both Mumi and
Papi were lying next to each other on their mattress,
one holding the other tightly.

My little brother Kasav and my cousin Jerry were
both snoring like tired, old men who had just
finished working a long, hard graveyard shift. I laid
back down in my cot and stared up at the rusty,
broken down one room shanty's ceiling, sweat
trailing down my face, thinking about **WHAT** I
remembered from my dream. It was the same dream
almost every night.

It was dark all around me, and I was floating on my
back in an ocean staring up at the sky. Instead of the
water being clear and blue though, it was pitched
black like an endless vat of used, burnt engine oil or
thick tar. In this ocean of thick, dark liquid, there

was a bunch of human bodies floating all around me. They weren't dead bodies, but they weren't alive either. They were just…. floating.

Everything was completely silent and serene, then suddenly, an intense bright light began to shine out in the middle of the sky. I shielded my eyes from the brightness. It started off small at first, but then began growing brighter and brighter until I could barely make out anything else around me. Before I knew it, my body started emanating the same light from the center of my chest, and soon my entire body shone brightly and searing hot until I couldn't take the heat anymore and began to scream with a blood curdling shriek. That's where the dream always ended for some reason, and I would wake up sweating as if I had just ran a marathon. I laid back down. As I stared up at the ceiling, my eyelids began playing chicken with each other and I was fast asleep again in no time.

Kockadoodle dooooo!

The rooster crowing off in the distance woke me up with a quick jolt.

"Looks like you're finally leve (awake). It's about time. I thought you had died in your sleep," my little brother Kasav whispered as he kneeled next to my little cot. Mumi and Papi had already awaken to tend to the farm out back and get the day started.

"The dream I had last night made me feel like I was dead. Like I was in another universe or something," I replied groggily.

"Same dream again huh? Wha-what do you think it means?" he asked almost hesitantly.

"I don't know…I honestly don't know." I murmured with a shrug.

I heard the rooster crow again for the last time, and then Mumi's voice replaced it with a loud, "Timoun! Vin deyò epi ede nou!" (Hey kids, come outside and help us).

I got up quickly and we made our way to the outhouse to brush our teeth using our fingers and some dried mint leaves. Jerry had already awakened earlier to go tend to the goats way off in the fields behind our house. He was one year older than me so as a result, he had more responsibilities that I did. He was more like an older brother to us that a cousin really. His mom and dad gave him up for adoption when he was a baby so my parents took him in as their own.

He has a younger sister on his mother's side name Dorothy who was pretty cool. She hung out with us whenever her parents came over to visit and was just like one of the boys. She wasn't afraid to get dirty, play with frogs, or even help us build traps to catch pigeons or rats and domesticate them as pets. Jerry's been our brother ever since I could remember and people would call him, Kasav, and I the Three Stooges. They called Jerry and I Tom and Jerry because we would be conniving and secretly planning mischievous things to do to each other. We did everything together, including getting in trouble. This was where our bond of brotherhood was forged.

Sometimes we would climb up these tall coconut trees near the beaches of Cité Soleil and try to see who could stay up there the longest without becoming scared and try to climb back down. I would always win because I wasn't afraid of anything. I would sometimes try to drop coconuts on top of their heads just to see if I had good aim. That cracked me up so much! Today though, Jerry wasn't around. Kasav and I went outside to help Mumi and Papi clean up the garden in the backyard.

"How long does it take to wake up and get out of bed?" Mumi asked me smiling.

"You know we have a dreamer in our family Bibi" Papi exclaimed.

"Did you have the same dream again Dodi?" Mumi asked with a worried look on her face.

"Yea" I responded.

My name is Dominique Salazar, but people who know me call me Dom for short. My Mumi called me all sorts of silly pet names that I hated, like I was still two years old! My family and I lived on this amazing island called Haiti, in a city called Port-Au-Prince. We lived outside the city center in a shanty town community called Delma off by the countryside. For as long as I can remember it has always been me, Kasav, Jerry, Mumi and Papi. Our grandmeré (grandmother) and grandperé (grandfather) lived a little ways off from us just over on the other side of the high hill we lived on. They were my mother's parents. My father's father passed away long before I was born so I never got the chance to meet him and his mother lived a good distance away from us so we barely ever saw her.

Our grandparents invited us to spend some time with them on the weekends so we can hear all of the amazing stories of how their parents grew up during African slave times and how much they had to go through as kids. I loved hearing those stories because I tried to imagine myself living during those times.

Sometimes, the things they would tell us about those stories made me so angry that I just wanted to cry. Then, there were those times they would tell us how our ancestors fought the slave masters and made them leave our island. I usually waited for that part so I could run around with a stick pretending to be a sword like I was Jean Jacques Desaline himself shouting, "koupe tét, boule kay!" (Cut heads, burn houses) Mumi would get so upset with me when I did that. She didn't want anything to happen to any of her kids. She was extremely protective of us.

Today was yard cleanup day. We lived on a nice area of land with lots of bunun trees (banana trees) and a few mango trees as well. We also had yams, tomatoes, corn, squash, greens, onions, and a few other fruits and vegetables. I really enjoyed spending time in the garden and outdoors. There's just something about nature that makes me feel at home, like I belong here on this planet. I probably spent a minimum of an hour a day inside our shanty. I really don't know why I didn't like being indoors. It seemed as though I was able to communicate to nature itself when I was out there in a sense.

Papi called me over to where he was to show me how to use the backhoe. I really looked up to him. This man, who stood five foot ten with a lean body frame and large gold rimmed glasses, was a professor at the biggest university in downtown Port-au-Prince, and he LOVED what he did. He had been doing it for as long as I have been alive and maybe even longer.

We were living during a time on our island where a man by the name of Jean Claude Duvalier was in charge the country. He was sort of like a president, but he had complete and total control of the country. He was a horrible and brutal leader. He had a group of militia policemen called the Tonton Makout that went around the country beating, torturing, and even killing anyone who didn't agree or believe in the ways of the government. I was really scared though that one day they were going to arrest Papi and kill him because he was and is still the most fearless man I've ever known who spoke out against any injustice or corruption he saw.

At dinner time, when we all would sit together around the cauldron, outside in front of our one room shanty, sharing some delicious diri blan ak sòs pwa nwa (white rice and black beans), he would tell us how Haiti needed to stand up against the tyranny, injustice, and oppression of this government we were living under and none of this could take place until we all remembered where we came from and what our ancestors did for us.

Like my grandparents, he would tell us of all the powerful people of the first successful African slave revolt in the history of African slavery, and how a few overcame so many. Those stories filled me with so much pride and love for my heritage and people that I would often wish that I was born during that time so I could fight alongside them. What did I know anyways, I was just a kid letting his imagination run wild I guess.

"Hey, are you going to just stand there, or are you going to help us with this yard?" Papi snapped at me to wake me up from my stupor.

"Oh, I'm sorry" I mumbled.

We were getting the garden ready to harvest the crops this evening. Today was my eighth birthday and it's probably my second favorite holiday of the year. The first one is January 1st, New Year's Day. That's when Mumi made her famous and tasty soup joumou (pumpkin soup). Probably the best in all of Haiti. The soup was actually cooked by all Haitians all over the island on this day to mark the day we took back our freedom and declared our independence from Europe a long time ago.

I began helping Papi rake up all of the weeds and dead leaves in the garden. A few of our neighbors were also outside in their yards tending to their crops. Our community was filled with so many kind and generous people. A typical day in Delma was filled with the sounds of kids running around playing with used car tires, old men sitting around a game of dominos, women washing clothes by hand and hanging them out to dry, and the smell of delicious Haitian food filling the air. If you were a stranger who happened to be walking down the street in our little village and someone spotted you, they would ask you if you've eaten anything for the day. Its best you responded with a yes, because if you said no, they wouldn't let you continue on your journey without sitting at their house and having a meal before you traveled on.

My father's mother, grandmere Elioca, was the most notorious hospitable person in the entire community. People would make sure if they were heading anywhere, that her shanty was the one place NOT to walk pass in front of. I saw her cuss a young man out one time because he politely turned down her invitation to come eat in her home. He looked so confused and scared at the same time! I couldn't stop laughing at him.

"When you're finished with the garden, I want to take you guys downtown to get some ingredients for your mother's cooking tonight" Papi disclosed to us while rubbing my head playfully.

Mumi gave him a weird smiley face look over her shoulder as she walked back into the shanty. I remember seeing that look between them before. Two months later, after that same look, they broke the news to me that I was having a little brother. Adults...sheesh!

"I bet you I can clear out all of the leaves and weeds faster than you can!" Kasav taunted.

"Think again dummy" I responded.

We both started plowing through the garden like two mad men raking for lost gold. After five minutes of scraping and scratching at the soft moist earth, we were done and panting like thirsty puppies. I won of course.

We raced each other back to the shanty from the garden and he redeemed himself of his previous lost by beating me there. As we walked in I could see Papi's face had changed from pleasant and peaceful to now anxious and serious. Mumi was standing across from him with her smile now gone and replaced with worriedness. He had RTNH (Radio Televizyon Nationale D'Haiti) radio on playing and quickly turned it off once he saw us enter.

"Hurry up boys and put your shoes on, we have to go get what we need downtown and get back home soon." he responded sullenly.

A small, ever present, and uncomfortable rock began to grow in the pit of my stomach. A rock that felt no bigger that a grape. I didn't know why or how it even started, but I could sense that it was there and it wasn't planning on leaving anytime soon. Kasav and I threw on our sapats (sandals) and made our way out of the house with Papi. Our destination: downtown Port-Au-Prince.

~Chapter 2~

Ou Paka Kache

(You can't hide)

Downtown Port-Au-Prince is freaking AMAZING! My eyes were immediately overwhelmed by all of the vibrant shades blues, reds, and yellows of the Haitian women selling handmade skirts on the road side or the illustrious greens and oranges of the tropical rain birds flying and squawking in flocks up above. I inhaled deeply the salty, sharp scent of the freshly caught fish from the fishermen blowing in from the nearby port, and covered my ears with a cheesy grin at the blaring horns of the Tap-taps (public transport bus) drivers that were trying to make it to their next destination in a hurry.

"HEY, WATCH WHERE YOU'RE GOING, FOUT! (Darn it)" Papi bellowed at a driver who narrowly missed us as we were getting ready to cross the town square major intersection.

"Papi, can we get some bonbon (candy) today?" Kasav asked shyly.

Papi ignored him and continued walking along with us holding both our hands in a hurried pace. We finally made it to the farmers market where it seemed as though every single human being living in Port-Au-Prince shopped there for their groceries. It was an absolute labyrinth of produce, meats, and other goods and products. If you didn't know your way around there, you **WOULD** be lost in no time. Papi finally found the booth of his favorite merchant who sold herbs and spices.

Her name was Madame Rachelle. An older, widowed woman in her late sixties with an interesting limp in her walk, Madame Rachelle was the most pleasant, joyful, and kindest person I ever knew. I once saw her catch a small boy, much younger than I am, trying to steal a small pouch of her brown mushrooms. When she asked him why he did it, he told her his mother couldn't afford to buy any because her crops were stolen by neighborhood bandits so he wanted to get her some to cook with. Madame Rachelle looked the boy square in the eye for what felt like an eternity, slowly let his go of his arm, grabbed a handful of brown mushrooms, and stuffed them in a bag. She handed him the bag, whispered something in his ears, and he immediately began to smile. Afterwards, he ran off, still grinning from ear to ear.

"Bonjou belle Madame!" Papi gleamed with a small smile.

"Jodi a se pa jou a Osvald" (Today is not the day

Osvald) she replied with a somber look.

"What do you mean?" he asked quizzically.

"You didn't hear what Duvalier was going to start doing around here?" she responded puzzled.

Papi dropped the formal pleasantries with her and gripped my hands a bit tight as his face became emotionless.

"Domi, take your brother and go play by the fish market right over there." He pointed not too far off from where we were. "I have to talk to Madame Rachelle about something."

That was odd. My dad never struck a conversation with Madame Rachelle for more than one minute when we came here and he never couldn't say anything to her that he couldn't say in front of us. That grape was now a golf ball.

I took Kasav's hand and we darted in the direction of the men tossing fish from their nets onto the marina platform and yelling at each other about prices, weight, and size. While knucklehead was sitting nearby on a small stool near the counters, mesmerized by the boat crewmates who were cleaning and scaling the catches of the day, I began to wonder off to the far side of the marina near the docks to see if I could catch one of those tropical rain birds.

As if I had just placed noise cancelling headphones over my ears, in an instant, I couldn't hear any sound anymore. I could see everything around me still happening, the fishermen tossing fish to the men on shore, the butchers prepping the fish for sale, and the people in the market a little way off exchanging goods for money, but I could hear absolutely nothing that was happening.

As though someone had their face next to my ears, I heard a distinct, subtle soft voice whisper in my ear, *"Pa janm bliye kote ou soti"* (*Don't ever forget where you come from*)

I suddenly became aware of where the voice was coming from. It wasn't from anyone around me. In fact, no one was around me. They were all gone. The fishermen, the butchers, the market shoppers and vendors, the birds. ALL gone. It was also no longer day time anymore, but night. I stood there almost hypnotically fascinated by the sudden changes around me. I was standing alone on the dock looking out towards the water now and the voice was much stronger and more pronounced.

"Pa janm bliye kote ou soti!"

The waves from the ocean began frothing back and forth aggressively underneath the dock as though hurricane level winds were causing it, but there was not a breeze in the air.

"Pa janm bliye kote ou soti!"

I looked down at the thrashing waves that was now splashing onto parts of the dock and there, right there, out in the distance of the ocean towards the middle of all the churning, crashing waves stood a dark human like silhouette figure. Human in the sense that it hand arms, legs and a head like a human, but it was all extremely disproportionate to one another. For some reason, I was not afraid of this figure in the distance. I lifted my arms almost robotically and pointed out towards the figure and it mirrored exactly what I did. I no longer had any control of my body. With trance like movement, I started walking out towards the figure and it began doing the same.

With the strength and force of an ox, I felt myself being pulled back off my feet as though I was moving through a vortex and there I was again on the edge of the dock being held by Papi who had pure fear and angst in his eyes as he looked down at me.

"What were you doing!" he stammered. "Didn't you hear me calling your name?"

I looked around confused and felt a bit dizzy. What was he talking about? Did he not just see what I just saw? Kasav was standing next to him, petrified as well.

Before I could utter another word, we heard sirens off in the distance. We all looked in that direction. *Someone must be hurt or have died in the market today,* I thought. I could see people begin running in all sort of directions. The fishermen began quickly packing the fish in crates and storing them underneath the docks in what seemed like secret basements. The closer the sirens got the more frantic everyone around us became. Papi grabbed our hands and began speed walking towards one of the alley streets we usually take to go home without looking left or right. *What was happening? Why is everyone in a hurry to leave so quickly? Aren't the sirens the ambulance?* I kept pondering as that speed walk turned into a light jog.

We reached halfway down the alleyway when I heard three loud *BANG, BANG, BANG!* followed by men shouting and women yelling in the direction of where we just came from. Papi and I were now in a full-on sprint with Kasav doing his very best to keep up with us. I've heard that bang before. It's the same one I would hear when the local bandits came through our neighborhood looking for things to take and they would take turns trying to see who could shoot as many of the stray dogs that roamed the streets.

"Don't…be afraid…. just…keep running!" Papi belted to us in between breaths, with a rigid yet comforting tone as we were running for what seemed like an eternity.

We were finally far away enough to where we couldn't hear the commotions or noise from the marketplace anymore. Papi stopped running and plopped down at the base of an oak tree we had come upon. Kasav and I did the same. We sat there in silence for a minute catching our breath and looking everywhere else but directly at each other. Kasav had a weary look on his face. I really love that kid. He was just a year younger than me but he always acted like he was older than me. He was a bit on the chubby side, so getting around seemed like a challenge for him. He would often ask Papi or Mumi to pick him up and carry him when we went out to town. He was so lazy.

"Papi, I want to go home to Mumi." Kasav pleaded.

"Ok, ann ale. (Let's go)" he responded.

We all stood on our feet, dusted ourselves off, and began walking back the rest of the way home. No one said a word or made a single peep as we walked. Kasav looked so weary, but he didn't utter a single complaint. We travelled through the forest with my favorite creek and finally made it back to our shanty just before the sun began to set off in the horizon. Mumi saw us off in the distance and began running towards us down the hill with her arms stretched out in front of her, dried tear stains on her face.

"Woy, bondye!" (Oh my god) she stammered.

"We're ok Bibi" Papi assured her as she held on to us all tighter than crab claws.

After kissing me and Kasav all over our foreheads for what felt like a million times, we headed up to our shanty. That night, as I laid in my cot, I could hear Kasav and Jerry snoring lightly next to me, their bellies full of the finger licking diri d'jon d'jon and koden fri (black mushroomed rice and fried turkey) that Mumi made for my birthday dinner. Granmere made her famous Haitian cake for me. She used fresh papayas as the filling. Kasav killed two huge slices by himself. That boy can eat! My birthday celebration felt different that year. Although everyone else around me was happy and joyful for me, something in me felt different.

Papi and Mumi were outside out-front sitting around a bonfire talking to each other. I couldn't make out the exact words they were saying, but I knew it was something important because I heard

Mumi shout at one point "NOU PA KAPAB!" (*WE CAN'T*) in a frightened voice. Their voice volume lowered completely after that and I couldn't hear anything else afterwards. You ever heard the saying that life is like a roller coaster, so hold on tight for the ride? Well, something told me that I wouldn't be able to hold on tight enough for what was to come.

That golf ball was now a tennis ball.

~ Chapter 3 ~

Lanmou chokola karamel

(Chocolate caramel love)

The morning sun's rays slowly crept its way up my sheet covers until they found my eyes and woke me up. I squinted at the light and glanced over in my brothers' direction. Jerry wasn't there again. Probably in the outhouse getting ready for school. Papi was already long gone to work at the university. Kasav was still under his covers snoring like a beaver. I sat up and gave him a nudge to wake up.

"Uhhh…" he muttered groggily.

"Wake your butt up man or we're going to be late for school" I insisted.

He turned over and waved me off as though I were a peasant. I'm was in the third grade, Jerry was in the fourth, and Kasav was in the second. We all went to the same primary school in Delma. It's a small private school with only fifteen kids and ran by a principal we all really loved. Her name was Madame Henriette. A tall, slender fair skinned woman with a curly light brown afro, hazel eyes, and a smile that seemed to make all bad things disappear in an instant. She spoke fluent French and used to live in France when she was a kid. She had a teacher's assistant name Madame Soleil that Jerry really didn't like and she didn't like him either. I never had an issue with her. Today was picture day at school and I didn't know where it came from, but my head began to hurt.

"Are you ok Dodi?" Mumi asked me lovingly as I was putting on my clothes while watching Kasav finally drag himself out of bed to get ready for school.

"No, I have a small headache" I responded.

"Do you want to stay home then?" she asked.

"Naah, today is picture day and I really want to get it over with." I responded.

"Ok cheri" she smiled.

Kasav finally finished putting his clothes on. Gosh he takes forever to do things! All three of us each grabbed a piece of fruit on our way out the door and kissed Mumi farewell. On our way to the school we ran into two of our neighborhood friends, Jeremy and Jerome. They were twins. They didn't go to school. Their parents couldn't afford to send them to school so they stayed home to work on the family farm and help out. They were the strangest twins though. Typically twins did the exact same thing and even finished each other's sentences. These two were like night and day, complete polar opposites and constantly at each other's throat.

"Sak ap fet neg! (What's up homie)" Jeremy motioned to Jerry.

"Nap boule fre! (Just hanging brother) " he responded with a high five.

"Hey Domi" Jerome muttered.

"What's up with you Jerome?" I inquired.

"This idiot of a brother got me in trouble with our pops yesterday for something he did, but I took the blame for It." he retorted.

They started arguing amongst each other while we continued walking to school. Night and day with these two. They finally stopped bickering like cats and we change the subject to something that made my face flushed with blood.

"Sooo, Domi, Jerry tells me he thinks one of the girls at Madame Henriette's school has a crush on you neg!" Jeremy teased.

"I don't know what he's talking about. **YOU** can believe that fool if you want to." I shrugged.

In all honesty, there was a girl at our school that I

had a huge crush on, but I didn't know whether or not she felt the same way. Her name was Sabine. We all wore uniforms at this school, but Sabine used to take it up a notch with her uniform. She would ALWAYS come to school with her hair done in cute pigtails, finished off with yellow and pink berets. She wore the shiniest black flats that matched her little black purse. To top it all off, she wore a different set of earrings every day, like she had one for each day of the week! When she spoke and the sound of her voice landed in my ears, I thought there couldn't possibly be any other sound in nature that sounded as heavenly as her. In other words, I became completely undone whenever I was around her so I did my best to avoid her when we were at school.

"Are you going to ask her to marry you man?" Jeremey continued teasing.

"Shut up koko be (idiot)!" I fumed at him.

We made it to the school and dapped up the twins as they headed back to their family's farm. I headed to class so that I could be the first one there.

"Bon jou (good morning) Madame Henriette!" I said sheepishly as I walked into class.

"Bon jou Dominique" she responded with that soft, comforting smile.

"How was your weekend?"

"It was ok, my birthday was on Sunday and my family celebrated it with me." I informed her.

"That sounds awesome!" she exclaimed.

As soon as she finished speaking, in walked Sabine! I hurried over to my seat, sat down, and began pretending like I was reading our textbook. I did not glance up once from my book but could see her in my periphery taking a seat in her chair. Today she looked like a bouquet of velvet roses peppered with an assortment of daisies and tulips all wrapped up with a pink ribbon. Gosh she's so beautiful! Why can't I seem to function when I saw her or was around her though? I mulled over in my head.

We got through our lesson rather quickly. Madame Henriette had us line up to go to lunch and recess afterwards. I didn't know why, but my headache was getting worse by the minute. I've had headaches before in the past, but this one felt very different. It was affecting my balance and I started feeling really nauseous. My head decided on a great day to start doing this. I thought. I met up with Kasav during lunch and we sat down to eat. I didn't say much.

"Hey, do you think you can help tell this girl that keeps trying to kiss me that I don't like her?" he begged.

Here I was trying not to internally combust when I was around my elementary school crush, and this kid is pleading with me to help him keep a girl off of him! Oh how cruel of a universe we lived in.

"Sure, I got you little bro." I mumbled.

This headache was at a point now where it felt like it was ripping my head apart and I began feeling extremely dizzy. Madame Henriette came out to the lunch/recess yard and began calling everyone to line back up so that we could start our picture day a bit early. I stood up and began walking over to where everyone else was and barely made it three feet when I felt as though I was on a merry-go-round, only, instead of me going in circles, everyone else around me started rotating around me. As the spinning began rotating faster and faster, guess who decided to walk up to me for God knows what reason. Sabine!

"Hi, you're Dominque right?" she asked shyly.

"Yea, I'...I'm...I'm..." I stammered.

The world around me by now was whirling like a washing machine with no off switch. I heard someone in the background ask in a muffled and slow motioned voice "Heeeyyy, arrrrre yyyyyyyou ooook?" Next thing I knew, I was throwing up every grain of rice, piece of turkey, and morsel of cake I ate the day before, and guess who happened to still be standing in front of me to catch all of it on her freshly ironed dress uniform and shiny black flats? I was so glad I fainted afterwards. At least I wasn't witness to my own social death.

I woke up blinking a couple of times to a blurry vision of a sky encircled by faces staring down at me. I blinked a final time, and those faces were now clear. The faces were my classmates. One of them was Madame Henriette.

"Dominique, are you ok?" she cautioned.

I didn't know how to respond. I just laid there. Helpless. I didn't see Sabine's face in the crowd of faces, which meant I at least still had enough time to go jump in the nearest river and drown myself.

"I think I am now Madame Heneriette." I muttered hesitantly.

"Alright petits enfant (little children), there is nothing else to see here, you may all go back inside now." she urged.

After Madame Soleil gathered everyone else inside, Madame Henriette helped me stand up off the floor.

"Do you still want to take your picture today? Can

you manage?" she inquired.

"Sure, I think I can." I quivered.

We walked back to the school building and for some reason, my headache was completely gone. I mustered up whatever bit of dignity I had left and managed to crack a weak smile for my picture. I didn't see Sabine anywhere around during the picture shoot. I just knew she thought I was the inconspicuous pile of dog poop you accidentally stepped on after having bought those favorite pair of brand new shoes you've been waiting forever to wear. After school, as I stood near the school entrance waiting on Kasav to get ready to start our two mile trek home, someone's figure caught the corner of my eye.

"Hi!"

It was Sabine! I held my breath so as to not respond with a shaky voice or let out any sound that mimicked an animal like an idiot.

"Heh-heh-hey" I shuddered.

"Are you feeling better?" she smiled.

All I could do was nod. She had on a different dress and some new flats. I could barely keep myself from fainting again as she continued looking at me with those alluring brown eyes that made me want to completely drown in them.

"So, I know we don't talk much in class, but I was wondering if you were going to take anyone to the upcoming school dance next week Friday." she asked.

Wait, WHAT!?! Did my burning ears, from all the rushing blood flow, just hear what my angel in disguise said? Did this goddess in human form really ask me out to our annual school dance? After I just blessed her with all the contents of my stomach? I finally regained control of my body and leaned over on the side of the school wall in an attempt to regain some cool points. I looked away for a bit as though I was in deep thought.

"No, I'm not taking anyone…yet." I boasted with a tiny grin in the corner of my mouth.

She caught my grin and started twirling one of her pigtails around and leaned in a bit towards me. I could smell her now. Gum drops. She smelled like gum drops or peppermints. I liked both of those. I began breathing a bit easier now.

"Well, if you're not taking anyone, did you want to go with me and maybe hang ou-?"

"Yes!" I shot back without letting her get another word out.

"Ok, no problem…I'll see you then!"

She turned to walk away but glanced over her shoulder back towards me.

"By the way, don't worry about what happened earlier today. It happens to me too sometimes when I get migraines." she exclaimed.

On our way home from school, Jerry, Kasav and I met up with the twins again. They were doing their usual bickering and teasing. I could hear them behind me as we were walking along side my favorite creek near the forest less than a mile away from home. As they were carrying on cackling, every square centimeter of my brain was occupied and filled with Sabine. What was this strange feeling I was feeling right now? As though I could climb up the tallest mountain or swim across the widest ocean.

Was this what Mumi and Papi felt for each other when they made those weird faces to one another?

Was this love?

~ Chapter 4 ~

Yo ka tande ou

(They can hear you)

Today my uncles Jude and James were coming to visit us and in pure excitement and joy I was running around the front yard all morning, doing cartwheels and attempting to climb the palm trees to jump off of them. Jerry was sitting on the floor at the threshold of our shanty front door and Kasav was taking a nap. Those were what his Saturdays were mostly filled with; that and eating. Jude and James were Mumi's older brothers. It was a real treat to have them come visit because they were both musicians and visual artist and they would teach me how to play a really groovy Haitian kompa tune on the guitar or a funky drum rhythm on the tumboo (congas).

They would also bring by some of their paintings to talk to us about what inspired them to paint the images. They too were against the government and their brutal rule over the people and often talked to us about a new Haiti, one without fear of being persecuted anymore. Finally free to live as human beings. They both also had locs that they started growing and it made them look like they were part of Bob Marley's band The Wailers.

Sometimes when they wanted to be mean, they would tell us spooky folktales and stories about the lou gaou (Haitian mythical creature) and how they would roam the island at night looking for small children to eat alive. Those stories would scare the living daylights out of Kasav, but made me tickle inside. I looked up to those two men a lot.

"Ey, ti gacon, sispun couri tankou on makak!" (Hey little boy, stop running around like a monkey) Jerry belted.

He did that often, acted like he was my older brother, even though he was only a year older than me.

"Jude and James are stopping by today man!" I replied out of breath. "I wonder what they're going to **DO** with us today."

"Well, you're probably going to be too tired to do anything if you keep running around like a mad man." he insisted. "Besides, don't you have to help tati (aunty) Carmel with dinner for later?"

For some strange reason Jerry referred to my Mumi as his aunt. Don't ask me why, I have no clue. Ever since we adopted him that's what he's always called her. I mean, technically she was his aunt, but because we loved him like a brother it always felt weird to me when he called her that. I ran around for another minute before I decide to go inside and help Mumi prepare for dinner later.

She was making poul fri (fried chicken) diri bluh and sous poi rouge (white rice and red beans sauce). Mumi's food was probably the best tasting food in all of Delma. She usually started prepping for dinner that day in the morning time.

"Jerry! Go get a chicken from the coup for me and get it ready please." Mumi called out to Jerry.

Prepping a chicken was the weirdest thing I've witnessed and still creeps me out to this day. I've only seen my uncle Jude do it once before. I remember it like it was yesterday. He went to the coup out back and grabbed one of the small hens. He then walked over to us holding the hen under his arm while simultaneously holding its head in between his thumb and first finger like a pool player holds a pool stick.

Then without any warning he began twisting the chicken with the hand that was holding its head in circles! Round and round and round he turned until......*SNAP!* Just like that, the hen's neck was broken. I think my stomach snapped at the same time because I felt a sick sensation all over my body and couldn't eat chicken for an entire month. Jerry did what he was asked to do with the chicken outside while I stayed inside until he was done.

"Mumi, do you know what time uncle Jude and James are going to be here?" I nagged.

"They told me they were coming by in the afternoon cheri, I don't know the exact time." she informed. "You know we don't care much about time around here."

She was right. In Haiti, if someone tells you they'll be coming by your place at a particular time, just add saayy three to four hours to that time, and that's when they'll actually get there. People weren't in a hurry much on this island. It may have looked that way on the surface or from the outside looking in, but trust me, we took things really easy around here. That's one of the many things I loved about my culture.

"Yea, you're right. They'll probably get here right before the sun goes down." I confirmed.

Jerry came inside and signaled to Mumi with his eyes that he had completed his deed. Mumi responded back with a small solemn nod and continued chopping vegetables. They often communicated like this to each other when he had to kill one of the farm animals we raised out back, whether it was a goat or a chicken. Come to think of it, many Haitians didn't say or express much around the topic of death. Funerals were a time of celebration, joy, and pouring of libations. That's when the elder of the village would take a bottle of water or sometimes alcohol and pour it on the ground after thanking the ancestors for having sent the spirit that had now moved on. I wonder what really happens to you when you die. I thought about death a lot when I turned six. It was the first time I ever witnessed it.

I was in the forest with my favorite creek laying on top the biggest branch of my secret hideaway tree. I was taking in the sound of soft, lulling water flow, while following the flight pattern of a bright blue and yellow butterfly across the tree line in the distance. I came here often when I wanted to escape from anything negative I was feeling or seeing around my neighborhood. No one knew where it was, not even Kasav or Jerry, so I could spend almost all day out there and not be bothered by anyone. I would be up in my tree watching below a mother wild boar taking her young to the creek for a drink or listen to the birds sing and try to interpret what they were saying to one another or calculate how long it would take the spider up above my branch to re-spin it's web from scratch. My own little oasis.

Suddenly, I heard some voices off in the distance. I sat up immediately to investigate and remained low and as still as an owl so I wouldn't be seen. It was three teen aged bandits trudging through the forest and they were fussing amongst themselves.

"I told you to stay out front and keep watch you koko be (idiot)!" the taller one growled at the shortest one.

"I was, I just had to go pee really bad and couldn't hold it any longer" he retorted.

"Fout (dammit), I don't care! You cost us a good lick." the taller one fired back.

They were all carrying rifles strapped across their shoulders and chest, and the taller one had a pistol in his hands waving it around as he was chastising the shortest one.

"Now we have to wait until later tonight and find another house way on the other side of Delma." the taller one continue. He kicked at a nearby bush in a fit of rage.

They all stopped talking at once and looked in the same direction. I looked in that direction as well because I heard what they heard. It was a small whimpering. I scanned the forest floor to narrow in on what it could possibly be. I saw what the noise was coming from. It was a small mongrel dog and it look like one of its legs was injured. He kept attempting to walk but was going in circles and would fall every three steps. The bandits began heading in the direction of the dog. They finally reached him and were standing right over it. The dog didn't seem to be aware they were there, because it kept attempting to walk on its hurt leg.

All three of them were just standing there, heads tilted, looking down at this creature as though it were a science project or an experiment. On their faces was a mixture of fascination and disgust, waiting to see what it would do next. I looked on with raw sadness. My heart began racing at the thought of what they were thinking in their heads to do in that moment. The tallest one glanced over at the shortest one and snarled,

"Next time you mess up our lick, this is what will happen to you."

He lifted the hand that was holding the pistol, pointed it at the exhausted animal, and pulled the trigger three times. I looked away with my fingers in my ears and cringed. I looked back, and they were all gone. The dog laid there motionless. I waited up in the tree for as long as I could, and once I was sure they were completely gone, I climbed down carefully and walked over to where it was laying. This living, moving, breathing being, a few seconds ago, was now as still and unflinching as a rock. No more whimpering, no more panting, no more pain.

I knelt down next to it, tears pouring down my cheeks, and began rubbing its head. *Why was I crying? This dog wasn't my pet,* I thought. I couldn't help it. I sat down with my legs crossed next to it, and continued petting its head until the sunlight began to fade all around me in the forest. Finally, I stood up and started gathering piles of fallen branches, palm leaves, and dried forest grass to cover it up while wiping away my tears with blood-stained hands. I didn't know why I was doing what I was doing. I had never seen it done before. It just felt like the right thing to do. I laid the last piece of palm leaf over the lifeless creature and began my hike back home as night finally caught up with me.

I hope someone will be there to rub my head when my body is lifeless one day.

Kasav finally woke up from his beauty sleep and came out back to see what Jerry and I were doing.

"Hey guys, is Papi back yet from work?" he grumbled.

Papi worked on the weekend sometimes to earn a little extra money. He normally took the three of us out to a movie theatre called Imperial downtown to watch American movies dubbed in French. My favorite movie was about this white guy who was really a robot underneath his flesh. I think he was from the future and was on a mission to kill this white woman. I had no idea why, but that human robot was so cool! I would pretend to be it sometimes by using Papi's black sunglasses and riding my chainless bicycle. Watching American movies was the one time I was able to see what it was like living over there. It seemed like an amazing place to live.

I used to hear older people talk about over there like it was a place next to heaven; where the street were clean, the food was out of this world, and you could do and become anything you wanted to be in this world. I never really paid much attention to those talks. I loved living in my country where I could be free to just…be. I was surrounded by nature, a huge family and close community, deep cultural connection with our ancestors, and we weren't too far from the beach.

Yea, I know that things were a bit unsafe because of the government we lived under, and we didn't have the best quality of life, but at least we had a life. I think Papi wanted to become the dean or president of the university someday, at least that's what I thought. Maybe if he became the president, we would be able to move out of our shanty to the other side of Delma, where the kids lived in actual houses and had real front yards with grass. I know, wishful thinking.

"No, not yet. James and Jude are going to be here soon so go see if Mumi needs help with anything." Jerry instructed.

"Yea, I think Mumi might need some help testing out the fire pit with a young plump boy to roast to see if it works properly!" I teased.

"Ha ha, real funny koko bey." he snapped back with a worried look on his face and went back inside to see if Mumi needed him for real.

He was so gullible. Jerry and I went back to chatting about the upcoming school dance, and who we were thinking about going with. I didn't tell anyone about Sabine and what happened at school. I wouldn't be able to live it down, especially with the fellas. They would make a huge fuss about it.

"So do you have anyone in mind to take to the dance man?" Jerry asked.

"Naw, I'm keeping my options open for now. I don't think I even want to go to that stupid dance." I lied.

"What do you think about me asking Maxine bro?" he inquired.

"You mean skinny Maxine? The one who snorts like a pig when she laughs?" I asked unsure.

"Yes" he confirmed, with a playful shove to my shoulder.

"I think she's pretty cool I guess." I lied again.

Maxine was the same girl who was going out with two boys in the same grade and neither of them knew about it. I could never understand why people did stuff like that. It didn't make much sense to me, but whatever, as they say, "to each their own."

Jerry and I chatted up a bit more out back until we heard Mumi shout from inside with joy. We knew what that meant; our uncles had finally arrived. We went inside, gave them both big hugs, and grabbed chairs for them to sit and take us on an adventure of Haitian culture, arts, and music.

That night, after our uncles were gone and everyone was fast asleep, I laid down in my cot facing up, staring at the ceiling, and pondering on what our uncles shared with us. They took us on a journey starting from Africa with the great civilizations that created most of the things we use and take for granted. They talked about mighty kings, queens, and warriors who fought off European invaders that wanted to control our ancestors. People like Queen Nzinga, and Hannibal the Great, or Queen Amanirenas. I was completely absorbed with their tales when they came and visited us.

As my eyelids became heavy and mind began to drift into dream land, I heard an unfamiliar sound coming from the tree line from the forest with my favorite creek just across the field of our back yard.

"*SSSSSsssssssssssssssGLOP*"

I sat up out of bed and crawled over to the far window as carefully as I could, so as to not make any noise and wake anyone up. I finally made it to the window and heard the noise again, only this time it sounded much closer.

"*SSSSSSSSSSSSSSSSSSGLOP*"

I reached my head up to peer over the window ledge, and when I was finally able to look outside across at the forest in the distance, what I saw made me freeze completely. I couldn't blink nor could I breathe. I could feel the pounding of every heartbeat in my ear drums. Up until that point, nothing really ever scared me, but tonight, I was absolutely petrified. Way across on the other side of the hill that we lived on, in the middle of the pitch-black forest, were two floating illuminated eyes attached to nothing, staring back at me.

~ Chapter 5 ~

Lamou se doulè

(Love is pain)

School was complete drag today. Madame Henriette was going over our arithmetic number line while I was counting down the clock on the wall until lunch and recess. Today, Jerry brought his football, which in other places I heard is called soccer, and I was filled with anticipation to get out on that field to show off my footwork skills. I L-O-V-E looovvve football! Everything about it fuels me. My favorite world team is Brazil. They have a player name Ronaldinho who is an absolute football god. He can do things with his feet and a ball that should be completely illegal.

The bell finally rang, dismissing us all to lunch. I spotted Kasav in the lunch line waiting to grab his desert and find a few of his classmates to sit with. I heard a voice behind me that made my knees buckle a bit.

"Hey you"

 It was Sabine. She had on a bright red blouse and skirt with red dangle earrings to match. She was smiling that heart melting smile at me again.

Don't say anything stupid Dom, don't say anything

stupid!

"Hi there" I smiled back.

"Is it me or is time moving extra slow today!" she exclaimed.

No, but your beauty has increased my heart rate, and I can't think straight right now.

"Things do seem to be taking a bit longer today" I affirmed her. "How's your day going so far outside of that?"

"I can't complain, I got an "A" minus on my quiz from last week, so that's a plus for me" she bragged.

"It doesn't surprise me at all that you got such a good grade; both beautiful AND smart!" I emphasized.

She began smiling extra hard and twirled her pigtail. Where did that come from? Both beautiful AND smart?!? Who was this person uttering those words? I didn't know where or how I got the confidence to say that to her, but wherever it came from, it was working in my favor. One of her friends came over tugged on her elbow.

"Come on Sabine, let's go sit over there with Janine and her cousin, they have some juicy stuff to tell us about you know what" she pleaded.

She waved at her and silently mouthed to me *I'll talk to you later* as she was walking away. I think I'm really starting to like this feeling now. It reminds me of the same feeling you get when you have something sweet for dessert after having a filling dinner. You don't want to eat it all up at once but instead take your sweeeet (no pun intended) time.

I started to turn around to head over to where Kasav was when *POW, SPLAAAAT!* I accidentally bumped into Mark, the oldest kid at our school, and sent his food tray flying in the air all over his pants and shoes. He never really said much to anyone around school. Kept to himself most of the time. We never really knew **IF** he was nice or mean kid.

That heart that was racing with love and good feelings a few seconds ago was now pumping with pure fear. All eyes in the cafeteria were glued firmly on me and the kid who I knew was getting ready to rearrange my face with his fist. He looked down at his pants almost emotionless, then back up at me, then back down at his pants again. Before he could utter a word, Madame Henriette was standing there between the both of us like she had teleportation powers.

"He shoved my tray out of my hands on purpose!" he declared.

"That's not true!" I yelled back.

"Ok, enough from the both of you." she hissed. "Mark, go to the front office to get cleaned up and you young man can go back to my classroom and wait there so we can discuss what happened here."

I turned around immediately and made a beeline out of the cafeteria, away from all of those eyes, which I know included Sabine's. I can't believe he lied like that! I now knew whether or not he was nice or mean. I slammed the classroom door behind me and sat next to the window overlooking the quiet, empty recess yard. I'm on the wrong side of life with possibly the meanest kid in school, and my crush had to witness it all. This day couldn't get any worse. Five minutes passed and the recess bell rang. I watched as all of kids from the cafeteria poured out into the recess yard filling it with shouts, laughter, screams, and....and.... football.

I could see Jerry organizing a few of the boys in teams and once he was done, a full game was underway. I watched him dribble past one defender, a second one, do a half turn pana in between the leg move that was sick! He was getting closer and closer to the other sides goal and I soon began shouting and cheering for him in the class as though he or anyone could actually hear me. I grabbed a rubber mallet off the windowsill and began chanting "go Jerry, go!" He finally reached the opponent's side and launched the ball in the far-left corner to secure the first goal of the game.

"Goooooooooooooooooooaaaal!" I gleamed with joy as I swung my arm in the air not realizing that the mallet I was holding had slipped out of my hands and flew right through the glass window with a loud *CRASH!* I stood there with my hands covering my mouth as if the sound of the window breaking came out of there. Everyone on the recess yard continued playing as though nothing had happened. Maybe it wasn't loud enough for them. I do know who it was loud enough for though. I heard a door creaking behind me and turned around to see a look of complete shock on Madame Henriette's face.

I was staring at the clock on the wall again, only this time it was in the school front office. Madame Henriette called Papi at his job. I could see her in her office from where I was sitting but couldn't make out what she was saying. They were on the phone for what felt like an eternity. Finally she hung up.

"You father said he's on his way to pick you up from school. I suggested to him that you spend the rest of the day at home reflecting on your behavior today." she scolded. "I have to say, I don't know what has gotten into you today Domi but I am a little bit disappointed in you and I hope you start making better choices after your reflection."

Goodness gracious, why is she acting like I just robbed the Haitian national bank!?! I didn't respond. After about fifteen minutes, Papi walked in the front door of the school. *Sigh, now I can go home with Papi and go to my hideaway spot in the forest with my favorite creek*, I thought to myself. Something didn't seem right though. Papi's face was devoid of any expression or gentleness. No, his face looked as though he was absolutely stoic, lifeless almost. He didn't even look at me. He shook Madame Henriette's hand, thanked her, and signaled for me to get up and walk out with him. That tennis ball in the pit of my stomach was now a bowling ball.

As we walked home side by side he said nothing to me. He kept his face forward in one direction but would periodically look up at some of the trees we passed underneath. I had never seen him behaving this way before. Why wasn't he saying anything to me? After a mile of walking, he finally broke the silence.

"I don't know what you were thinking today, or why you decided to behave the way you did, but I swear to you it will be you last time." he snarled.

As we were passing by a tree with some low hanging branches, he stopped dead in his tracks, reached up and broke off a lengthy size branch. He started frantically pulling the leaves off as I stood there dumbfounded by what he was doing. *Was he going to try to make fire with those, out here, right now?* I thought, and before I could finish that last thought, he swung the hand holding the branch with all of his might and landed it square on my back.

I felt as though my back had just caught on fire and as a knee-jerk reaction I attempted to grab at my back and run away, but he grabbed onto my arm and held me there as he continued swinging that thick branch over and over on my back. Every lash more painful than the last. I did my best to hold my breath so as to not yell in agony, but my mouth wouldn't betray me. He finally stopped, dropped the branch, looked me squared in my eyes overflowing with tears, and let go of my arm.

We continued making our way home. My back was in so much pain, it felt cold. I could feel blood trickling down and soaking through my shirt whenever it rubbed against it. We finally made it home, and Mumi greeted us at the door concern written all over her face. Papi walked in right past her and straight through to the back yard while

Mumi pulled me inside with a hug. She didn't ask any questions or make any comments. It was as though she already knew what had just taken place. She turned me around in her arms to investigate my body and see where the injury took place, and when she saw my back, she gasped and began to cry. We were both crying now. She mended my wounds with some gooey aloe Haitian remedy, wrapped my back up, and walked me over to my cot to lay down.

Right before I drifted off, I tried to grapple in my mind if the same man that I looked up to and saw as my hero, the same man who I was proud of and wanted to be like was the same person who caused me that much pain without an ounce of remorse or emotion on his face. The same man whom I now had a fear of.

The last thing I saw before my eyes finally gave way was my mother kneeling down on her knees in front of her bed with her hands folded.

~ Chapter 6 ~

Leve

(Wake up)

I stopped screaming. I no longer felt any pain. Instead, I was enveloped in pure comfort. The same comfort your feet feels when you stop for a moment to rest, after having walked a few miles on unpaved roads barefoot. The black ocean was gone, and I was now on an open plain with tall light brown grass and some weird twisted looking trees off in the distance. There was a light warm breeze blowing across the grass and it smelled like cinnamon. It wasn't day, or night, but both, with the sun and the moon on opposite ends of the horizon. My mind couldn't make much sense of it. My entire body was still emanating light that was now slightly pulsating. I looked down to examine it, but it wasn't there. In its place was a form that resembled a cloud or very condensed smoke. I reached down to feel what it felt like and realized that I had no arms.

Suddenly I heard a voice I had heard somewhere before.

"Pa janm bliye kote ou soti."

I looked up and way off in the distance, standing near the tree, was the same dark disproportionate human-like figure I saw out on the ocean. In the blink of a thought, I was standing directly in front of the figure looking up at it. It was as tall as the twisted tree it was standing next to. It had no defined features on it that I could describe. No mouth, no nose, no ears, just pure black. Almost as black as the universe with illuminating eyes. It looked down at me and tilted its head slightly to the side as though it was curious.

"Never forget where you came from my child. You are light and love. Share them both freely but protect them fiercely." it whispered.

I started to respond to it, but realized I had no mouth to speak through. I thought to myself, *how was I supposed to understand what any of this meant?* when it replied back,

"Do not worry, I know all your thoughts. **YOU** *will understand when it is time for you to understand. For now, do not fear pain, embrace it. It is not the enemy of pleasure. It is necessary. In your other form, you will endure a lifetime of it. Stay the course, do not give up. Many will not understand you. Many will try to eliminate your light. Shine brighter. Shine stronger. Shine longer. Subdue all fear."*

I stood there, well, floated there for what felt like a

million years. The figure slowly turned around and began walking away.

Wait, why me? Why do I have to be so different? Why do I have to go through it all? I thought.

The figure continued walking away slowly and responded without turning back around,

"Because I am."

What in the heck did that mean?!? Before I could ponder some more on what the figure said, I was instantaneously transported back to floating on the black ocean again, only now it was aqua blue as though I was back on Earth again. I was in my human body and began treading the water to stay afloat. The sun was shining high in the clear blue sky, and there were a couple of seagulls gliding nearby, squawking at each other. The dark figure was gone, the light brown field of tall grass was gone, and I was all alone, out in the middle of this endless ocean, treading and floating, waiting on something to come and rescue me from the empty vastness in every direction.

~ Chapter 7 ~

Lumou dou

(Love is sweet)

Today was the best, worst day of my life. The school dance was later this evening and I was filled with a surge of energy and anticipation to be going with my caramel angel Sabine. I was also meeting her father today, which made me want to find the nearest, biggest boulder I could find, and hide underneath it for the rest of my natural life. I don't know why I was afraid to meet him. Oh, wait...maybe it was because of the fact that he was the country's secretary of treasure under the dictator Duvalier, and the senior bank manager at Unibank S.A., the largest bank in Haiti. In other words, her family was rich rich, while mine on the other hand was dirt poor.

Mumi was really excited for me that I was taking her to the dance. She was running around the shanty frantically looking for materials to use to hem up my dress pants and iron out my chemiz (button down shirt). Papi was at work, and Jerry was out in the field tending to the goats. Kasav was in the front yard playing with one of the neighborhood stray cats. My back had healed up pretty quickly since that day. I did my best to avoid Papi though whenever he was around. Whenever he would reach out to rub my head like he normally did, I'd flinch a little. I couldn't help it.

"Is she a pretty girl?" Mumi inquired as she was sewing up my pants.

"Mumi! Can you please not ask me that?" I pleaded.

"Whaaat! I just want to make sure she's pretty so that I know how your children will look" she teased.

Is this really a thing that parents do? Find the most embarrassing thing to think of to say or do to you and say or do it anyways. I hope I don't ever put my future children through the same torture. I went back to reading the book that my head was buried in. I glanced over at Mumi from the edge of my book. It made me feel really good inside to see her when she was smiling and happy. Especially if I was the source of her happiness. There was a bright twinkle in the corner of her eye when she was genuinely happy. This was how I knew when and when not to ask her for something I wanted. It was also apparent that when she would talk to herself, she was not in a good mood at all and to stay clear of her. She helped me pick out a bouquet of beautiful Camellias' to give Sabine tonight and I didn't want anything to happen to them. I placed my book down and went out front to see what Kasav was doing with the neighborhood strays.

"Hey, what are you wearing to the dance tonight?" I

asked him.

"I don't know. I didn't want to go but Mumi wants me to even though I'm not going to be with anyone." he declared.

"Wellll, I'm sure Maxine will be there so maybe your mind will change when you see what she's wearing." I informed him.

"I don't care if she had on a pink bikini with her booty all out, I'm not doing anything with her, not dancing, not holding hands, and not doing anything!" he specified.

"Okay, okay, jeez." I conceded.

Was this his way of expressing that he really like her deep down by pretending that he didn't? Boy, this love thing was really starting to seem as complicated as I heard it was. Mumi was finally finished repairing my pants and ironing my shirt and called us both inside to get dressed. Jerry decided he wasn't going to go tonight. He wanted to go hang out with the twins' downtown. I don't know, but he seemed to be hanging out a lot with them lately.

Well, Kasav and I were ready to make our three-mile journey to school. I was going to be meeting Sabine's father at the dance. She lived way up on the hill on the other side of town, where all the well to do

Haitians lived. There was no way I was going to meet her up there. Me? A poor, disheveled kid from the slums of Delma? Walk up to the front door of a national diplomat's house to pick up his daughter for a date? Fat chance!

Kasav and I kissed Mumi goodbye and started on our trip. We briskly made it through the forest with my favorite creek and crossed the Bourdon Hills. We passed some stacked burning tires on the side of the road and what appeared to have been a charred body inside. Kasav didn't notice it so I felt relieved. He didn't respond well to death.

We finally made it to our school building. As much as we tried not to get dirty on our way there, it was practically impossible. Our black shoes were covered in dust and mud when we arrived at the building, so I told Kasav to follow me to the boys' bathroom so we could clean ourselves up as best we could. The great thing about our situation was that we were almost an hour early. We found the bathroom and got ourselves situated.

"Hey, you've got some dirt on the back of your pants, let me clean it off for you." I suggested to him.

I cleaned him off and made sure he was good to go. Once we were confident that we were clean enough, we left and headed to the cafeteria. Of course the first face we ran into was none other than Madame

Henriette.

"Bonsoir, Domi & Kasav, welcome!" she beamed. "You two are the first ones here with about twenty-five minutes to go before we start."

She pointed us in the direction of the sitting area and informed us that we could wait there, but to not eat or touch anything from the snack table. I could see the instant sadness in Kasav's face. We headed over to the waiting area and sat down as instructed. The cafeteria looked so different. There were bright green banners stretched across all the walls. Blue and green streamers were hanging down from the ceiling and a huge shining disco ball was hanging down the middle of the lunchroom I assumed where the dance floor was. There was streaking lights shining all over the walls, and floor, and the lights were dimmed down. The D.J. was playing some pretty nice zouk and kompa rhythm over his loudspeakers which made me start tapping my feet to the beat. I couldn't help myself sometimes when it came to music. When Uncle James and Jude would show me how to play the tunbou (conga), I would go crazy with some funky beat combinations that made them sit back in amazement.

I had become so lost in the music the D.J. was playing, I didn't realize that the clock on the wall read six o'clock, which meant the dance was officially underway, and I could see kids start to trickle into the lunchroom. There was one kid who walked in and seemed to be searching for someone all throughout the cafeteria. It was Sabine! She finally found who she was looking for, and motioned for me with her hand to come over to where she was. I walked over to where she was and felt like I had just taken a sip of the cleanest, coldest, and most refreshing spring water after being near death on the Sahara.

"Hi!" she exclaimed waving at me sheepishly with that sweet smile.

"Hi! You look amazing!" I insisted and immediately handed her the flowers.

She took them and began twirling her pigtails.

"Hey, there's someone I'd like for you to meet." she informed me.

Oh no, I thought, *here goes nothing.*

We walked over to where her father was standing, with his back turned, speaking with another parent and Madame Henriette. She tapped him on the shoulder and he turned around to investigate who summoned him.

"Papa, I'd like you to meet Dominique. He's one of my classmates and friend." she informed him.

He looked like a character I once saw in this American movie. It was about a police officer who was brutally shot and almost killed by a group of bandits, well, at least that's what they looked like to me in the movie. This police officer was taken by a big scientific company which kept him alive to replace the parts of his body that was missing with robotic machine parts.

Her father examined me like a painter would a blank canvas before they began brushing colorful strokes onto it. I stood there everywhere else except directly in his eyes. Finally, after being apparently satisfied with what he was standing in front of, he reached out his hands to shake mine. I looked up at him and reached out to shake his hands.

"Pleasure to meet you young man. You show my daughter a good time tonight, just not too good." he affirmed with a sinister smile as his hand grip became tighter. I honestly thought I heard a bone or two in my hand snap like a piece of wooden ruler.

All I could do was nod and keep from yelping out in pain. He let go of my hand, kissed her on the forehead and walked out without as much as a single glance back. *So that's what the hands of a rich, power-hungry man felt like,* I thought. There was something about him though that didn't feel right.

"Come on!" Sabine gushed as she grab my throbbing

Jell-O hand and pulled me out onto the dance floor. The D.J. dropped some Carimi, so it was either show her that I had some moves or go sit in a corner somewhere. So, I did what any smart boy would do when challenged by the love of his life to dance; I got funky with it. We danced to some fast-paced kompa for what felt like an eternity. She twisted, turned, and twirled like I never seen before.

There's a saying we have in Haiti that goes *Koh ou di sa bouch paka pale (The body says what words cannot).* Right now, her body was saying all KINDS of things that my mind was trying it's best to understand, but my own body wouldn't let me do much thinking. After a few upbeat tunes, the D.J. finally changed the pace and slowed it down to some slow troubadour. I started to walk off the dance floor thinking she was going to do the same, but she grabbed a hold of my now less throbbing hand and pulled me back closer to her. *Oh no…what is happening right now? What do I do? Oh gosh, I hope I don't step on her feet!* I rummaged over in my panic-stricken mind.

She held onto my hand and guided it around the small of her back. *Gulp!* She then took my other hand and clasped it into the softness of hers and held it just above our elbows, all the while looking up at me with a look I hadn't seen before. *Gulp, gulp!* It was the same look Mumi gave Papi when she asked him to help her do a task around the house and he did it without any complaint.

We were about a foot and a half apart from each other, when almost like magic, our bodies began gravitating closer towards one another until we were both pressed up against each other. *Gosh her body felt so warm!* I gushed over in my mind. She laid her head against my shoulder like a baby would after being full and comforted. Her hair smelled like citrus fruit, coconut oil, and lavender. I inhaled slowly to take in all of that heavenly scent so that I didn't seem like a weirdo.

Without a single warning, sign, or even heads up, she reached her head up and planted her soft glossy lips firmly on mine. A surge of electricity shot straight from my lips all the way down to the tip of my toes and back up again and I pressed mine against hers more firmly.

We stood there, in the middle of the dance floor, with the rest of the world completely melted away and replaced by the melodic vibrations of musical energy, flowing all around us, through us, within us. Time came to an absolute halt. I could have been wrong, but for a moment there, just a brief moment, it sounded like our heart were beating in perfect unison.

Just like that, we pulled our faces away from each

other and were staring into each other's eyes. She looked away, slightly smiled, and laid her head back down on my shoulder as we continued dancing.

If this was a part of the whole love thing, I **COULD** feel this way forever.

~ Chapter 8 ~

Je pense, donc je suis

(I think, therefore I am)

I instantly cracked my eyes wide open and laid as still as possible. There was a strange sensation on the side of my face. The sensation started at the bottom of my neck and continued up the side of my face as I laid on my stomach in my cot. *Wait...are those tiny legs?* Yes! It was a huge cockroach taking a hike up my face and it seemed to be in a hurry. I jumped up with lightning speed, slapped it off my forehead, and heard it land on the floor with a loud *PLUFF!* It scurried off like its life depended on it and was gone before I could even thing to grab a shoe or sapats (sandal). I felt an immediate rush of disgust wash all over me and almost threw up in mouth.

My commotion stirred Kasav and Jerry a bit from his deep lumber chopping slumber. I laid back down to see if I could fall back asleep, but the psychological damage had already been done. I sat back up, looked over at the boys to see if they were fast asleep again, and headed outside to the backyard. I was met outside with the blaring sound of the village rooster crowing. The sun began to illuminate the night sky with a deep burnt orange tint off in the horizon. I located a dry pile of hay we used to feed our goats and laid down on it. The soothing final orchestra score of chirping crickets started to lull me back to sleep again like a ballad. *One two three, chirp two three, one two three, chirp two three.*

I was awaken again by a different sensation on my face. This time it was one of the goats licking me.

"Arggh! Get away from me kabrit sal (dirty goat)." I shoved its face away, squinting at the sun's annoying ray.

"Looks like someone couldn't sleep last night huh." Jerry announced as he grabbed his shepherd staff to get his day started with his belting four legged friends.

"What time is it?" I inquired.

"Ten past nine." he informed and started herding the goats out to pasture.

I sat up and looked around like a drunkard watching him get further and further away. I sat there a little while more and my mind shifted back to my exhilarating experience last night. My first kiss ever, and there were no words to describe it. I licked my lips a bit to see if I could still taste her lip gloss. *Mmmmm, cherry.* Madame Henriette was going around taking pictures of everyone at the dance and snapped a nice shot of Sabine and I with her Polaroid camera. She gave me the copy. I handed it to Sabine for her to keep, but she insisted that I hold onto it.

We looked like we knew each other since birth in the pic, both of us smiling and beaming with so much joy. Today was another Saturday, and I was contemplating whether I should hang out in my hideaway tree or stay around our neighborhood and play with Kasav and Dorothy who was coming by later. I decided to isolate myself and think some more about what I was feeling inside for Sabine.

"Good morning Dodi, what happened? Why are you outside cheri?" Mumi consoled as she poked her head out the back door.

"There was a ravèt (roach) crawling on my face." I informed her.

"Ohh, I'm sorry cheri. Ou bon? (Are you ok)?" she comforted.

"Yea, I'm going to my safe place in a little bit." I informed her.

She gave me a loving glance and went back inside to make breakfast. I finally stood up, brushed the hay off myself, and went to the outhouse to do some hygiene. Papi was at work today again. We seemed to be drifting apart further and further in our relationship.

Whenever I saw him now it was either when he was getting ready to leave for work, or when he was getting ready to lay down to sleep at night from a long day of work. If he ever did speak to me, it was to give me an instruction or direction. It was strange considering how much time I used to spend with him before.

I devoured my breakfast in less than two minutes and was out the door heading to my hideaway tree. On my way to the creek I spotted the twins just of the edge of the forest heading towards what looked like downtown and waved at them from a distance. They waved back and continued on their journey. I resumed mine as well, and along the way, I picked up and pocketed a few shiny, neat stones I saw on the path.

I made it at last to my tree, carefully climbed up to the comfy branch, and laid back to take in nature. After about five minutes of the cool gentle breeze rustling through the forest canopy, the mid-morning birds singing their blissful tunes, and a belly full of delicious Haitian laboui bunun (plantain porridge) I drifted off into the subconscious unknown with the events of last night being the last thing on my mind.

Shhck...shhck...shhck.

I didn't know how my ears were able pick-up certain sounds around me, but this one in particular woke me up. I sat up slightly and began scanning the forest floor in the direction the noise was coming from. I found the source. *Were my eyes deceiving me on purpose?* I marveled in my mind. I squinted to **SEE** better. It was Sabine! I rubbed my eyes like a mad man trying to make sure I wasn't still asleep or dreaming which I wouldn't have minded at all if I was. What was she doing way out here? How did she get out here all by herself? How did she know about my secret safe haven? My brain was running a million miles an hour now. I didn't move a muscle and watched what she would do next.

After walking for a few feet she came to a stop about twenty feet away from my tree. Her hair was out of the pigtail and laying loose on her shoulders. I sighed silently as I thought about running my fingers through them. She looked around a few times to make sure the coast was clear and that she wasn't being followed I guess, and walked over to a small bush off to the left of the tree I was in. Keeling down slowly, she reached under the bush, rummaged around for a few seconds and pulled out what looked like a book. She hugged the "book" tightly, gave it a kiss, and sat to start reading it. I scratched my head in wonder. *She came all the way*

out here just to read? She didn't have any libraries
in her rich mansion on the hill?

In my inner babbling of puzzlement, I didn't realize
I shifted my legs slightly to get more comfortable,
and one of the stones I had in my pocket fell out and
landed right next to her feet.

I froze like Medusa herself had just given me the
death stare. She looked around at first, and then
naturally lifted her head up to see where that object
came from. I pulled my head back a little, but it was
too late. She stood up immediately.

"Hello? Anyone there?" she inquired. "I know how
to fight and sling a rock so you better come out."

Say something you idiot, show yourself so she
doesn't become scared. I reached my head out in
full view and waved down at her as nonchalant as I
possibly could.

"Heeeyyy doowwwn theerrre!" I bellowed casually.

"Wait, Dom-Dominique, is that you?" she asked
peering up the tree.

"Yeess, I'll beee doowwn in a feewww." I shouted
down.

I climbed down as slowly and carefully as I could
so that I didn't make a complete fool of myself by

falling out of this tree or lord know what else.

When I finally made it to the ground, she dropped the book and immediately pounced on me with a tight squeeze. I grabbed a hold of the tree trunk behind me to brace myself from falling at the unexpected warm greeting. I hugged her back and we stood there for a few seconds holding each other. All of the feelings I had last night began resurfacing again, but even stronger. She finally let me go.

"What are you doing out here and up in a tree?" she inquired with the biggest smile on her face.

Don't you dare tell her the truth, you'll look like a dummy. She'll think you're a complete weirdo.

"I come out here when I want to get away from any stress or issues I'm dealing with. I climb up the tree to keep hidden from anyone passing by underneath and from any wild predator animals too" I insisted. "The more burning question I've got for you thought is what are YOU doing out here?"

She looked away sheepishly and her smile faded a bit.

"I come out here…for this." She grabbed the "book" that she started to open up and look at. Only it wasn't a book at all. It was a family album.

"My mother died when I was a baby and my father told me that she killed herself. I've kept these pictures of her as a way to connect with her but also…" she hesitated, "my father has forbidden me to have any pictures or things of hers around the house. He said that she was a coward and took her life to leave us here by ourselves. He said that she was selfish and he didn't want anything around the house to remind him of her."

I continued to listen without speaking.

"Something just doesn't add up though. If your wife did something like that, why would you want to forget about her? Why not keep her memory alive by having pictures around of her around to remind you of the love you had for her?" she insisted. "I come out here because this is the only place I know I can get lost from all of his bodyguards he keeps around me almost twenty-four seven."

I grabbed her hand and pulled her towards the tree trunk.

"Do you want to see my hideaway up there?" I pointed.

"Um…I don't know" she murmured.

I looked her deep in the eye, "do you trust me?"

She paused for a moment, smiled again, and gripped

my hands tight.

"Yes" she affirmed.

I grabbed her album and placed it inside the waist of my pants. I turned around, kneeled, and motioned for her to climb onto my back. She did. I paused for a moment, advised her to hold on tight. She whispered in my ears, "always" and I slowly began my accent up the tree grabbing every vine and branch extra tight.

We made it to my hideaway branch at last and she climbed off.

"Gosh it's so unbelievably gorgeous up here." she declared as she panned the entire forest from left to right.

We looked through her mother's photo album. I could see where her beauty came from. After we were through, we sat up there side by side staring off into the tree line, counting how many of the Sun's rays we could see piercing through the leaves and branches. Our world became void of all external worry, anxiety, fear, or doubt. As we exchanged stories about our lives and experiences, space and time no longer mattered. We laughed, cried, and shared another exhilarating kiss that sent a slight pulse wave of energy wave throughout the rest of the forest that was so powerful, the birds began singing their delightful songs to one another.

"Oh, no, I have to go," she cautioned.

"Ok" I replied.

We climbed back down and I walked her as far as I could to the edge of the forest. She grabbed me again for a hug and turned around to continue on the rest of the way home.

I got back home just as the night sky became filled with stars to find Papi sitting out front near the outhouse shed. I increased my pace to make my way in the shanty.

"Domi, come here, I want to show you something," he beckoned.

I stopped, looked around to see if I could spot what he was trying to show me before I walked over to him, and started heading in his direction. When I reached him, he pointed up towards the sky.

"You see that group of stars off in that region there?" he indicated. "They are called the little dipper."

"You see those right over that way?" he continued. "They are called Orion's Belt."

Um.... why was he showing me this right now...?

"You see this group allll in this area here?" he emphasized. "That group is call the constellation of Virgo. This is the constellation that represents the month you were born in. September tenth. It is the constellation of peace, justice, harvest, and celestial love. I don't want you to become lost in this world son." he continued. "This world is filled with unspeakable darkness. A darkness that will utterly destroy you if you're not wise. I want to you to know that you are light. Don't allow the darkness to consume you."

I continued to look at him as he spoke.

"When you were just four weeks old, your grandmother, your mother's mother, tried to kill you by poisoning your baby formula. I'll share the details with you another time. I know the other day I did something to you that I've never done before. I did what I did because I don't want you to let yourself be fooled by the darkness. Do you understand what I am saying?"

I nodded my head quickly so that I could just go inside, get in my cot, and go to sleep.

"Don't let anyone destroy your light son......not even me." he pointed at himself.

He reached over to rub my head. I flinched a little and he caught it. He kissed me on the forehead and sent me off to bed. As I laid in bed, I mulled over what he said to me in complete confusion. *What was this darkness he was talking about? Why would my grandmother want to kill me?* Thoughts of our conversation was soon replaced with thoughts of Sabine.

Why DID her father not want her mother's memory to remain alive...?

I drifted off.

~ Chapter 9 ~

Tan ou fini

(Time is up)

Papi seemed a bit more quiet than usual this Monday morning. He kissed Mumi goodbye and was out the door and off to work. Us boys also kissed Mumi goodbye shortly after and were on our way to school. We arrived at school, and the boys went their separate ways. I walked over to the school bus area and sat on a nearby bench. I was waiting on Sabine to be dropped off so I could walk her to her class. Her father's limo pulled up at the end of the parent drop off curb and she stepped out.

Waving her father goodbye, she made her way towards me. The smile she normally wore was a deep sad frown this morning.

"Hi bibi" I exclaimed.

"Hi" she mumbled.

"Everything ok?" I continued concern.

"I hate this STUPID school, I hate these STUPID clothes, and I hate my STUPID life!" she yelled, and without any warning, completely broke down in tears. I caught her in my arms before she completely let go of herself on the floor and held her there as she trembled with deep sobs seeping through my dark blue polo shirt. Thank goodness no one was around us at that moment.

She wept on my shoulder for the better part of three minutes, then slowly began to calm down. I let her go and reached into my backpack to give her the handkerchief I kept just in case I needed to wipe sweat from my forehead on long walk home.

"Thank you" she whimpered.

I nodded and remained silent, waiting for her to say whatever her heart wanted her to utter. After a few seconds of silence, she shuddered her words,

"My father found out that I've been sneaking out of the house, *sniff,* but he doesn't know where I've been going, *sniff,* so he added extra bodyguards to monitor my every move, *sniff,* which means I can't leave and meet you at our special place anymore. What do I do? *sniff,* I don't want to be away from you Dom!"

I stood there trying to contain my growing anger and rage inside. I didn't know what to do in that moment. Part of me wanted to be that half human half robot police in the movie I saw, and head up to that mansion to scare the living crap out of him and his bodyguards, but another part of me wanted to run far, far away from here with her and never look back. She laid her head back on my shoulder and began crying again, but only more subtle. *I have to find out why he doesn't want to keep her mother's memory alive,* I fumbled over in my mind.

"Hey cheri (honey), listen, I'm here for you and I'm not going anywhere." I assured her. "Let me walk you to the restroom so you can clean yourself up a bit, what do you say?"

"Okay, *sniff"* she whispered with a hint of a smile.

That made my anger subside a little. We walked inside the school building through the crowd of other students and found the nearest bathroom. She went in, and I waited for her outside. I saw Madame Henriette coming towards me down the hall and immediately turned around so she wouldn't spot me. The last thing I wanted was for her to get involved in any kind of way.

The way she was talking to Sabine's father the night of the dance didn't seem like it was a parent and teacher having a conversation per say. She continued walking past me down the hall. *Whew!* At last, my Haitian princess walked out of the bathroom looking much better than she did when she went in. I walked her over to her class, stole a kiss on her cheek when no one around was looking, and headed to class.

The day seemed to be moving along pretty quickly. During recess, I met up with Jerry and a couple of the other boys on the yard. Jerry brought his ball to school again, so we got a quick game of football underway. I was on Jerry's team so he and I were like the Haitian sensation football duo simply dominating the field. I would score a goal, then he would, and back and forth we went on as the other team scrambled to make just one.

It was game point, and Jerry had the ball underfoot. He dribbled past one defender, passed the ball to me and jetted towards the goal. I sent the ball screaming up in the air in his direction, and he leaped in the air to head strike it into the goalie's net. I jumped up with joy, but that joy soon turned into terror as I saw his feet miss his landing while he was coming down and landed headfirst on a parking lot space barrier. *THUNK!* He laid there completely motionless.

I zoomed across the concrete yard to where he was and all I could see was bright red blood sprinkled all over the pavement near where his head laid. Two girls on the other side of the recess yard who saw it all unfolded squealed in horror.

"Jerry, Jerry, hey, hey, you ok man?" I begged as I gently turned him over.

In the middle of his forehead was a hole about the

size of a little marble, and I could see a piece of what looked like was his brain inside the hole. I felt sick. His eyes were rolled in the back of his head and he began shaking uncontrollably. Madame Henriette, Madame Soleil, and one of the school safety officers made it over to where we were and I was shoved aside by the officer as he reached underneath his body to carry him back into the school building.

I wanted to follow them, but Madame Soleil held me back as well as some other kids who were out on the yard with us. I spotted Sabine way off coming around the side of the school building with her friends and ran over to her.

"Jerry's been injured." I panted frantically, pointing towards where the officer carried him.

"Oh, my god, is he ok?" she inquired.

"I don't know. They wouldn't let me follow them inside." I stammered. "If anything happens to him…" I trailed off with a buildup of tears forming in the wells of my eyes.

"Hey, hey, come here," she held her arms out to hug me. "He's going to be fine ok, don't worry, I'm right here."

I returned the hug, tears streaming down my face

now. *Why did it seem like whenever something good was happening to me, there was something bad just lurking around the corner?* I deliberated in my mind as *I* was the one now being comforted.

The sound of sirens caught my ears. I let her go and headed inside the school to see what was going on. I saw Madame Henriette standing in the doorway of the front office with some paramedics moving around inside the room. There seemed to be a small commotion going when finally she stepped aside to let them out. They had Jerry on a gurney with his head wrapped up in heavy gauze. He wasn't shaking anymore, but still he wasn't moving either.

The paramedics exited the building and a couple of the kids followed them outside, including myself. They loaded him up in their ambulance and were off with their sirens blaring again. I couldn't take it. I started running. I ran down the front steps of the school building, past the school gate entrance, and out onto the street. I ran…and ran…and ran until I couldn't hear Madame Henriette's shouts for me to come back anymore, or the sound of the other kids yelling my name. I ran the entire way home and only stopped when I saw Mumi out front hanging some clothes out to dry. I collapsed as soon as I knew she had made eye contact with me.

I woke up a few hours later in my cot and looked

around. Mumi was sitting on her mattress and came over to me when she saw I was up.

"Hey my pot, how are you feeling?" she probed.

"I don't want any more bad things to happen to me, to us." I began crying again. "I just want to be happy, I want us to be happy."

"I understand." she assured in her soothing calm voice. "I know what happened to Jerry today. Madame Henriette sent a messenger earlier. He's doing fine. He's at L'Hopitale General in stable condition."

The news slowed my crying down almost to a complete stop. She wiped them away and continued.

"I have **YOUR** dinner ready, do you want to eat something?" she asked.

"I'm ok, no thanks." I responded.

"Let's wait until Papi gets home from work so we all can go visit him in the hospital. Would you like that?" she asked.

I nodded. She looked at me with a smile, rubbed my head and began singing a really old nursery rhyme lullaby she used to sing to me when I was just a few years old.

"Savez-vous planter les choux
À la mode, à la mode
Savez-vous planter les choux
À la mode de chez nous."

I closed my eyes and left the world that seemed to be falling apart all around me.

The sound of loud voices woke me up with a startle. It was dark out, and Papi and Mumi were out back talking to each other but in a way I'd never heard before. Kasav was sitting on his cot playing with a few marbles in his hands with a blank look on his face. He looked like he had been crying.

"What are they talking about?" I inquired.

He continued playing with the marbles.

"Hey, did you hear me? What are they talking about?" I persisted.

"We're leaving." was all he said.

"Leaving? Leaving where? What the heck are you talking about?" I sat up confused.

Mumi and Papi's conversation ended abruptly and they both came back inside.

"Mumi, what's going on?" I asked.

She paused for a moment and glanced over at Papi

with sheer plastered all over her face.

"MUMI, what's going on?!?" I persisted, now standing up.

"We're…we're leaving Haiti in two days." she stammered with her head down.

Wait, what?!? What was she talking now talking about? Leaving Haiti to go where?!? Why?!? The room began slightly spinning. I sat back down before the spinning got any worse.

"What happened? Why are we leaving?" I begged.

She began talking. Today at Papi's university, a few Toton Makout's stopped by to make sure that no one was teaching or preaching anything anti-government or pro-democracy. Well Papi and his colleagues were doing just that during one of his extended afterschool programs and they walked in on it. They beat up a few of his friends in front of him, put a gun to his head, and told them to never step foot in the university again. Papi left immediately. So now with no job, and a government that had him on their radar we couldn't stay here anymore. It was too unsafe for us. As Mumi continued talking, I began to experience something strange I had never felt before; I felt no emotions. No anger, sadness, frustration, fear, no anxiety, nothing. It was like my entire emotional power plant had just completely shut down.

"So what does that mean for Jerry, and where are we going?" I demanded.

"We're going to America, to a place called Miami, Florida. I have a friend there who is helping me get a visa to fly all four of us out of the country. We'll be staying with him until we can get on back on our feet. Jerry will stay in the hospital here until he's fully recovered, and once he's at one hundred percent, we'll have your uncles bring him over." Papi declared.

Whoooa! Hold up! America!?! Flying? On a what, kite? Was this really happening right now? What was this Miami, Florida place like anyways? I never even heard of it or seen it before on any of the American commercials on TV. What about the forest with my favorite creek and hideaway tree? What about my school? Classmates? Nothing made any sense right now. I looked over at Mumi, and her head remained bowed. Everything in my life seemed to be crumbling into nothingness. Like in one of those action movies with a car chase scene. You know, as one of the cars careens left and right through traffic to avoid getting caught but manages to accidentally run off a cliff, and as it's falling in slow motion, you know as the viewer there's no way in heck anyone survives that crash.

This is what my life felt like right now but even worse.

Oh gosh…what about Sabine.

~Chapter 10~

Lakay se kote ke ouye

(Home is where the heart is)

Life has a fascinating way of forcing you to grow up even when you fight tooth and nails to try not to. Today was the day we were set to fly to Miami, Florida. We didn't have much when it came to things so we all shared two luggage for all our clothes. I didn't go to school yesterday because Papi had already sent a message to Madame Henriette that we were leaving the country to seek asylum in America.

While Mumi was looking around the shanty to see what else she could squeeze into one of the luggage, Kasav was out back playing around with the goats. He didn't seem too bothered this morning. He barely spoke a word during breakfast. Papi went downtown to the U.S. Embassy to make sure that our visa was cleared and that our flight was still secured. I gave Mumi a kiss and told her I was going out to the forest with my favorite creek. She pulled me in close for a hug and whispered in my ears, "Give her my love."

I looked up at her confused and immediately saw in her eyes what she meant. *How did she know?* I wondered. I gave her a small grin and left to head out to my hideaway tree for the last time ever.

The cool autumn island breeze flowed over and the down the hill side we lived on, reminding me of how comforting nature could be when things seemed bad. I stopped in my tracks, closed my eyes, and let the wind blow up against my face. I eventually made it to my tree. I looked around in the hopes that I would hear her voice or smell her hair from a distance. Neither happened. I waked over to the bush where she hid her mother's album in, knelt down, reached underneath and began rummaging around with my hands to see if I could feel anything.

It was there! I wonder why she left it. I grabbed it and climbed up my tree with it tucked in the back of my pants waist. When I got a top my safe haven, I pulled the album open and began flipping through the pages looking at her mother's pictures. I touched one of the pictures of her as a baby and her mother holding her on her waist with my hand. A tear drop landed softly on the clear plastic covering, then another. I stayed up there for as long as I could flipping through the same pages over and over again. After my last flip through, I pulled our school dance pic out of my pants pocket and kissed it. I slid it in one of the last empty plastic sleeves towards the end of the album.

I climbed back down and placed the album safely back where I pulled it out from. As I was getting ready to turn around and make my way back home, a blue and yellow butterfly caught my attention. It was flying in a pattern I had never seen before. It was as though it was floating to a slow melodic rhythm or music effortlessly. I followed it across the forest line until it was no longer in sight. I smiled and wiped my face off.

As we were boarding the plane in the terminal, I was the one now who was having a hard time keeping up with Papi and Mumi. I was trying to take in the new and unknown environment while my mind scrambled to create a safe **FUTURE**. The people speaking over the intercoms, the rolling luggage carts, the police dogs patrolling, the thunderous rumbling underneath my feet of the plane engines coming from the runway outside, locking into my memory the last things my senses would ever experience of my home, my Ayiti.

Easter egg hunt question: _____ _____ _____
____ ____ _____ _____ _____ _____
_____?

Answer: (Space given here for readers to answer the question)

ABOUT THE AUTHOR

Dommartini Salien, Sr. (aka Martini), is a first-generation immigrant from the island nation of Haiti. He migrated to United States in the late 80's with his parents and younger brother by way of South Florida. Martini completed K-12 in South Florida, and later went on to enlist in the U.S. Army as a Logistics Specialist in 2003.

After serving ten years in the armed forces, two tours in Iraq, being stationed on two continents, and traveling the world, Martini decided to complete his military career in 2012 and pursue his undergraduate degree while simultaneously working for multiple companies in corporate America.

 After completing his degree, Martini received a calling to make a huge career shift by becoming a middle school educator teaching brown and black kids in underserved communities. He pursued his graduate degree in business administration to launch his non-profit organization A.N.N. (Amazing Never Normal, Inc.) which gives brown and black kids vocational skills if college is not a practical route. Martini has been an educator for a total of six years and currently lives in Bronx, New York with his wife.